My Book of

Moral Stories
A Premium Collections

Book-9

Contents

Compiled & Retold by :
Nidhi Jayshree

1. THE KING BOAR

Once, a woodcutter brought home a wounded little boar. The boar had fallen into a pit dug for catching wild elephants. The woodcutter medicated the boar and after a while the boar had gone stronger and healthy.

The woodcutter took the boar back into the forest and left him in the area from where he had taken it.

The boar was soon hungry and had to hunt for his food. Suddenly, a wild tiger pounced on the boar in an attack. The boar somehow managed to kill the tiger. After that, the boar roamed into the forest and soon found his friends. He narrated the story to his friends. His friends told, "Is this the real story? A cunning fox had fooled us by telling that he was the one who killed the tiger."

The wild boar got really angry. He went in search of the cunning fox and killed him fiercely. When the fox had tried to escape by climbing on a fig tree, the boar had actually uprooted the entire tree.

The boars in the area assembled together and had a long discussion. At the end they concluded that the wild boar was strong and powerful. Hence, he was very apt to become their king. They went to the wild boar and said, "Hey strong friend, we have unanimously decided that you are the most eligible person to lead us and protect us from danger. Please be our king." After a long pause of thought the wild boar accepted their offer.

The boars joined together and made the boar to sit under a fig tree. They coroneted him as king and offered him sacred water in a conch shell, as a mark of respect. From then on it had become customary for a person to sit on a fig throne and be offered with sacred water in a conch shell while he is coroneted as king.

Moral : Even a powerful enemy can be destroyed through deceit.

2. TWO FREINDS

Lucky and Curse were two friends. Whenever they went together, the villagers mocked at them. "Hello Lucky! Why are you roaming with Curse? His name is so negative. So should be his character." Although Lucky did not mind this, Curse felt very bad.

Once, when Lucky was out of station, his house caught on fire. The villagers were afraid to go near and quench the fire. It was Curse who bravely fought the fire and quenched it. On his return, Lucky heard the whole story.

He took his friend Curse proudly and said to the villagers, "Look at who saved my house. It is Curse my friend. What is in the name? It is in the character that someone is good or evil. Don't ever evaluate a person by name."

Moral: NAME DOES NOT REFLECT CHARACTER

3. TWO IDENTICAL BIRDS

Two parrots of the same breed went to two different persons. One was a sadhu and the other was a criminal.

The sadhu used to pray every day morning, "Ram, Ram. Save the world." The parrot, living with the sadhu, also learnt to repeat the prayer.

The criminal used to scold and utter bad words right from morning to night. The parrot, living there, also learnt to use bad words.

One day, the parrot that lived with the sadhu wanted to meet the other one. It flew all the way to the criminal's house. The moment it set foot there, it heard loud scolding and bad words exchanged harshly from the parrot there. It could not believe its ears. So, it convinced the parrot to join with the sadhu, and exchanged places.

Now, the criminal started hearing the prayers, "Ram, Ram. Save the world." The parrot that had gone to the sadhu also started to hear the same prayer. In due course of time, the criminal turned good and his parrot also turned good.

Moral: GOOD WORDS BRING GOODNESS

4. THE ANTELOPE'S FRIENDSHIP

Once, an antelope got trapped in a hunter's net. He tried as hard as he could. He could not free himself. He started to panic and cry. A woodpecker heard the cry.

She wanted to help the antelope. She flew to a nearby pond and asked the animals there, "Please come with me to help an antelope that is trapped." Only a tortoise was helpful. The woodpecker asked the tortoise to gnaw at the noose of the trap and flew to the village in search of the hunter's home.

The hunter was fast asleep. In the mean time, the tortoise gnawed away the noose and freed the antelope.

The woodpecker was happy that she could help a fellow creature.

Moral: SELFLESS HELP IS SERVICE TO GOD

5. BITTERNESS

There was a wise king who ruled the ancient kingdom of Banaras. He was getting old and weak. Time had come for his son to take the throne, but the king was worried at the cruel and unworthy acts of the youngster.

The king pleaded with the Rajguru, "Hey learned Acharya, please teach my son good values and kindness. Reform him. He needs to be shaped to be able to take the throne." The Rajguru accepted and started teaching the prince good things.

A few weeks later, Rajguru and the prince were strolling in the palace garden. The Rajguru picked up a tender leaf from a small plant and asked the prince to taste it. The prince had just put the leaf in his mouth, and spat it out and started growling with sourness in his mouth. "Rajguru, what is that leaf? Why is it so sour?"

The Rajguru patiently replied, "See my son, if such a tender leaf itself is of foul and tasting so sour. Imagine how sour it would turn when it becomes older and matured!" With a Wise smile, the Rajguru left the place. The prince had just learnt his lesson. He became so kind and wise and ruled the kingdom to his father's expectation.

Moral: WISDOM ALWAYS PAYS

6. THE SAINTLY HARE

A hare happened to live near a monastery. He saw the penitence of the hermits there and started to practice it. He used to meditate just like the hermits and follow the rites and rituals they adopted. One evening, as the hare sat to meditate, he happened to see the full orb of the growing moon. At once he recollected, "Tomorrow is the fifteenth day of the growing moon. It would be a full moon day. I should be on penitence and eat only after I can find some saint and offer them food." The next day, the hare was awaiting some saint to pass that way. But, to the hares despair no one came that way. In distress, the hare said to himself, "I shall offer myself as food, if some saint comes."

The Forest Deity was watching the entire episode. He appeared in the form of a Brahmin in front of the hare. The hare was happy that his penitence is to be fulfilled. "Hey Brahmin, I had resolved to serve myself as food for the saint who comes here. So, please wait a few minutes. I shall jump into the pyre and then you shall eat me." Saying this, the hare jumped into the pyre he had set earlier. The Forest Deity was pleased by the dedication of the hare and gave back his life and blessed, "You are a truly pious creature. You shall go to heaven and live a sacred eternal life there when your time comes."

Moral: SINCERITY IS VIRTUE

7. THE CROW AND THE JACKAL

This is a famous story that has been told for years and years. It is about a <u>crow</u> that was cheated the way he cheated someone else. An <u>old lady</u> was selling some delicious dough rings. The <u>crow</u> stealthily hopped and stole a dough ring and flew away to a far away tree. The <u>crow</u> thought to itself, "How stealthy am I! I can eat this dough ring without any disturbance here."

At that very moment, a <u>jackal</u> happened to pass that way. He sniffed and caught the smell of the dough ring. Up on the tree, he saw the <u>crow</u> perched and about to savour the sweet dough ring. A plan struck the jackal.

"Hey crow sister, you are such a beauty. Your black feathers and the cute beak are breathtaking," the jackal started flattering. The <u>crow</u> started to faint in the flattery. The <u>jackal</u> added, "Oh! I love to hear your voice." The <u>crow</u> opened her mouth to sing, but alas, the dough ring fell down and the jackal ate it all and left the place.

Moral: CHEAT NOT, ELSE, YOU SHALL BE CHEATED TOO

8. THE GOLDEN DEER

In a forest valley lived a variety of strange deer. They had attractive golden skin. The skin was so shiny that it looked like real gold. Abu was a hunter who lived in a nearby village. He had heard plenty of stories about the golden deer. He wanted to catch at least one such golden deer.

Abu roamed all across the forest in search, and finally found them grazing in a remote valley. He set some traps and waited. When the golden deer herd came that way, one deer fell in the trap and got caught. At once, the deer shouted, "There are traps in this area. Everybody leave." On hearing this caution all other deers ran away from that place. However, the deer's brother and sister did not leave. They started mourning, "How can we leave you dear brother? We shall all stay together till the end of life."

Abu, who was witnessing all this, felt very emotional and set the golden deer free. Abu had learnt the value of true love and affection.

Moral: TURE LOVE HAS NO EQUALS

9. THE WOODCUTTERS AND THE SAL TREE

The trees in the forest had a deep discussion. "All birds build their nest on us and make us dirty with their excretions," complained the Fir tree. "It is true," accepted all trees in unison. "Not to say only that, even animals climb on us making scratches all over our trunk. This really stinks. We have to drive away all ," added the Sal tree.

A wise banyan tree opposed, "Look friends, life is interdependent. We need them for our safety and life. We should not chase them away." No other tree listened. The trees in the forest decided to chase away all birds and animals. The next day morning all trees shook so violently that the birds and animals who were resting both on the trees and beneath the trees fled away in fear. The trees were very happy. "We are free now," hooted them.

A few woodcutters came that way. They saw the big Sal tree and said, "At last, we are free to cut this tree. Till now there were many wild animals and birds living here. We were afraid to come here. Now that there are no animals and birds, we can do our work."

The woodcutters felled the tree and cut it into pieces. The other trees could do nothing but watch in despair. "Look, this is why I told you not to chase away the birds and animals. They are our helpers and protectors," emphasised the banyan tree.

Moral: SELFISH DEEDS LEAD TO MISERY

10. THE FALCON AND THE QUAIL

There was a big falcon. He was very powerful and strong. He could pick up very large animals in his claws and fly high and long. He was a terror to smaller birds, as they became his prey if they crossed his path.

Once, a small quail happened to cross his path. The falcon looked at the quail and said, "Hey small one, I give you one chance to escape. Fly as far as you can. If you can evade me I shall spare your life"

The poor quail flew as far as he could and landed on a solid rock. No sooner had he set foot on the rock, he heard the harking sound of the falcon shrieking in his ears. "Here I come," shouted the falcon in pomp and dived straight at the quail.

The quail waited till the last second and suddenly ducked away. The falcon, who came sweeping at the quail could not control his plight and hit hard on the rock and died immediately. The quail sighed in relief.

Moral: SIZE IS NOT MIGHT. WISDOM IS MIGHT

11. THE DONKEY IN LION'S HIDE

Once, a lion had died and its skin dried off. A donkey that happened to pass that way accidentally fell on the skin. The skin clung to the back of the donkey. The donkey strode into the village.

People got frightened by the strange looking lion. They could not recognize the donkey. People ran hither and thither in their fear. They were shouting, "Don't go near the animal. It is terrifying." The donkey got bolder and started to dance and hop. He frightened small children and youngsters. Parents ran to their children and took them to safety. Seeing all this made the donkey merry.

In his joy, the donkey opened its mouth and started braying loudly, "You fools! I am a donkey. See how I have cheated you." Although people did not understand the donkey's language, they immediately identified the voice of the donkey.

"Hey it is just a donkey. Come let us teach him a nice lesson," came forward a villager with a big stick and thrashed the donkey. They poor donkey now understood that it cannot imitate other animals.

Moral: APPEARANCES ARE DECEPTIVE

12. REAL EVIDENCE OF GRATITUDE

Marshal was a owner of a vineyard. He brewed high quality wine there. Many flies used to fall in the wine. Marshal used to collect them with care, dry their wings and when they were able to fly, he would let them free.

Once, a competitor filed a fake case against Marshal. The case came to the court. The witnesses were all decorated by the competitor. So, they all gave false statements against Marshal. The judge finally asked, "Marshal, do you have anything to say?" Marshal said, "Your Honour, I have no witnesses on my side, but, I am innocent." The judge replied, "How is it possible to count on your words alone against so many witnesses?" and was about to write his judgement.

At that moment an army of flies came buzzing into the court and surrounded the judge. They made patterns in the air as a symbol of Marshal's innocence. The judge was astonished at the act. He understood that Marshal was innocent and liberated him from the case.

Marshal was thankful to the flies for being his true witnesses.

Moral: KINDNESS IS REWARDED MANIFOLD

13. THE MONKEY AND THE DOLPHIN

Once a group of sailors set out to sea in their sailing ship. One of them brought his pet monkey along for the long journey. When they were far out at sea, a terrible storm overturned their ship. Everyone fell into the sea and the monkey was sure that he would drown. Suddenly a dolphin appeared and picked him up. They soon reached the island and the monkey came down from the dolphin's back. The dolphin asked the monkey, "Do you know this place?"

The monkey replied, " Yes, I do. In fact, the king of the island is my best friend. Do you know that I am actually a prince?"

The dolphin knew that the island was isolated. She said, "So you are a prince! Now you can be a king!" The monkey asked, "How can I be a king?"

The dolphin went away, saying, "As you are the only creature on this island, you will naturally be the king!"

Moral: PRIDE BRINGS PAIN

14. THE RABBIT AND HIS FRIENDS

Bunny was a lively rabbit. He was always in the company of some animal or the other. He was friendly with all of them.

Once, Bunny heard a pack of hunting dogs in the forest. He was afraid that they would catch him. He ran to a deer he thought was his close friend and said, "Dear brother, I hear a pack of hunting dogs in the forest nearby. Please save me. You have such sharp antlers. You can thrash them. Please help me, friend!" The coolly replied, "I am sorry, Bunny. I am too busy to help you out. Go and find someone else for you help."

Bunny ran to many of his friend – the bear, the monkey, the zebra, and even the panther. They all gave the same reply. Finally, the tired Bunny met a mouse and told his pathetic state. The mouse replied, "Why are you panicking. Just get into your borough and stay inside till the pack leaves this area. You shall be safe." Bunny went happily.

Moral: A FRIEND IN NEED IS A FRIEND IN-DEED